THE CLEANER

Copyright © 2024

All rights reserved

No part of this book may be reproduced, stored in a retrieval system, or transmitted in any form or by any means, electronic, mechanical, photocopying, recording, or otherwise, without the prior written permission of the publisher, except for brief quotations embodied in critical articles and reviews.

Contents

Chapter 1: The Secret Basement 1

Chapter 2: The First Job 4

Chapter 3: Learning the Trade 6

Chapter 4: The Detective's Suspicion 8

Chapter 5: The First Clue 10

Chapter 6: The Cleaner's Challenge 11

Chapter 7: Collins's Determination 12

Chapter 8: The Ongoing Battle 13

Chapter 9: The Legacy 14

Chapter 10: The High-Profile Cases 15

Chapter 11: The Presidential Cleanup 17

Chapter 12: The Detective's Breakthrough 18

Chapter 13: The Art Gallery Heist 19

Chapter 14: The Unseen Footprint 20

Chapter 15: The Tech Mogul's Secret 21

Chapter 16: The Detective's Obsession 22

Chapter 17: The Socialite's Dilemma 23

Chapter 18: The Near Miss 24

Chapter 19: The Cleaner's Masterpiece 25

Chapter 20: The Detective's Revelation 26

Chapter 21: The Unseen Battle 27

Chapter 22: The Presidential Clean-Up 28

Chapter 23: The Detective's Final Play 29

Chapter 24: The Cleaner's Escape 30

Chapter 25: The Legacy Continues 31

Chapter 26: The Billionaire's Secret 32

Chapter 27: The Relentless Pursuit 33

Chapter 28: The Diplomat's Dilemma 34

Chapter 29: The Detective's Discovery 35

Chapter 30: The Corporate Cover-Up 36

Chapter 31: The Final Confrontation 37

Chapter 32: The Legacy 38

Chapter 33: The Ghosts in the Shadows 39

Chapter 34: The Unsolvable Puzzle 40

Chapter 35: The Journalist's Curiosity 63

Chapter 36: The Confession 66

Chapter 37: The Final Job 68

Chapter 38: The Unseen Battle 69

Chapter 39: The Disappearance 71

Chapter 40: The New Identity 72

Chapter 41: The Legacy 73

Chapter 42: The Call 74

Chapter 43: The Return 75
Chapter 44: The Confrontation 76
Chapter 45: The Future 78
Epilogue 79
End of Book One 80

Chapter 1
The Secret Basement

Jack had always thought his life was ordinary, if not a bit strange. Living in a cemetery with his father, they maintained the grounds, cleaned the graves, and kept to themselves. Their home was a small, two-story house that sat on the edge of the cemetery, surrounded by ancient trees whose branches creaked in the wind. The house was old, with creaky wooden floors, a musty smell, and an aura of mystery that Jack had grown used to over the years.

Jack's father, Thomas, was a man of few words. He was tall and lean, with a perpetually stern expression and calloused hands that spoke of years of hard work. He never talked much about their family or past, but their life was simple and peaceful. Jack spent his days attending school, helping his father with the cemetery work, and exploring the vast, quiet grounds. Despite the eerie setting, Jack found solace in the tranquility of the cemetery.

Everything changed when his father died unexpectedly. It was a cold, gray morning when Jack found him lifeless in his bed, a look of peace on his face. The shock of his father's death left Jack reeling. He was left alone with no family and no idea what to do next. The funeral was a small affair, attended by a handful of distant relatives and a few neighbors who offered their condolences before quickly departing.

One rainy evening, while he sat in their small house, a phone rang. It wasn't his phone, but his father's. Jack picked it up and answered, but there was no response. Confused, he noticed a faint sound coming from the basement—a place his father had always forbidden him to enter. The sound was faint, almost imperceptible, like a whisper calling out to him.

Driven by curiosity and a sense of desperation, Jack ventured downstairs. The basement was dark and musty, filled with old furniture covered in dust and cobwebs. He fumbled for a light switch and eventually found it, illuminating the room in a dim, yellow glow. There was a door at the far end, but no handle. Jack felt around, punched the wall in frustration, and by sheer luck, he hit a hidden square that opened the door.

Inside was a room filled with weapons, cleaning supplies, disguises, and a wealth of items Jack couldn't identify. It was meticulously organized, just like his father always was. There were rows of shelves lined with bottles of chemicals, stacks of neatly folded cloths, and an array of tools that looked both familiar and foreign. Guns, knives, and various other weapons were displayed on one wall, each one carefully labeled and maintained.

On a table stood an old book. Jack opened it to find a message from his father, explaining that their family had a secret profession: they were cleaners, professionals who made murders look like accidents or suicides. His father had been training him unknowingly his whole life, and now it was Jack's turn to take over.

The revelation left Jack stunned. Memories of his father's seemingly odd instructions flooded back—lessons on how to clean meticulously, the importance of leaving no trace, and the countless hours spent learning how to repair and maintain various tools. Jack realized that his father had been preparing him for this role all along.

As he sat in the dimly lit basement, surrounded by the tools of a trade he never knew existed, Jack felt a mix of fear and excitement. He knew his life would never be the same, but he was determined to honor his father's legacy.

Chapter 2
The First Job

With trembling hands, Jack answered the phone. A frantic woman, Clara, had killed her husband and didn't know what to do. Her voice was shaky, and she spoke in hurried, panicked whispers. Jack could hear the desperation in her tone, and it stirred something within him.

Following his father's instructions from the book, Jack calmed her down, got the necessary details, and assured her he would handle it. He was terrified but also felt a strange excitement. The book detailed everything he needed to know—how to approach the scene, what tools to bring, and the exact steps to follow to ensure a clean job.

Jack gathered the tools and supplies from the secret room, reviewing the steps his father had laid out in the book. He packed a duffel bag with gloves, cleaning agents, a variety of tools, and a set of disposable clothes. He knew he had to be meticulous—no fingerprints, no hair, no trace of his presence. He practiced the techniques his father had described and set out to Clara's house.

The drive to Clara's house was tense. Rain poured down, and the windshield wipers struggled to keep up. Jack's mind raced with thoughts of what awaited him. He parked a few blocks away and walked the rest of the distance, the cold rain soaking through his clothes.

At the crime scene, Jack's nerves almost got the better of him. Clara opened the door, her eyes wide with fear. She led him to the living room, where her husband's body lay sprawled on the floor, a pool of blood spreading out around him. The scene was chaotic—overturned furniture, shattered glass, and signs of a violent struggle.

Jack took a deep breath and got to work. He methodically cleaned the blood, disposed of evidence, and rearranged the scene to look like a robbery gone wrong. He wiped down every surface he touched, careful not to leave any trace of his presence. He worked quickly but meticulously, following the steps outlined in his father's book.

It was his first job, and though it wasn't perfect, it was good enough. Clara was relieved, her gratitude evident in her tearful thanks. As Jack left her house, he felt a mix of exhaustion and exhilaration. He knew he had found his new calling, and despite the fear and uncertainty, he felt a strange sense of purpose.

Chapter 3
Learning the Trade

Determined to improve, Jack immersed himself in learning. He studied forensic science, watched crime documentaries, and read books on criminal investigation. He spent hours in the basement, practicing hiding his fingerprints, avoiding leaving hair or fibers behind, and erasing any sign of his presence.

Jack's next few jobs went more smoothly. He cleaned up after a jealous lover's quarrel, a business dispute turned deadly, and an accidental overdose. Each time, he refined his techniques, becoming more efficient and less detectable. He began to understand the psychology of crime scenes, how to mislead investigators, and how to make murders look like accidents or suicides.

Jack's reputation as a cleaner grew. He started receiving calls from a variety of clients—people from different walks of life who found themselves in desperate situations. With each job, Jack's confidence grew, but so did his awareness of the risks. He knew that one mistake could lead to his capture, and he was determined to avoid that at all costs.

Jack's routine became a carefully orchestrated dance. He would receive a call, gather the necessary details, and plan his approach meticulously. He would arrive at the scene, execute the cleanup with precision, and leave without a trace. He kept a low profile, avoiding any unnecessary attention, and made sure to stay several steps ahead of anyone who might be looking for him.

One evening, after successfully cleaning up a particularly challenging scene, Jack sat in the basement, reflecting on how far he had come. He realized that his father's training had been more thorough than he had ever imagined. The skills and knowledge that had seemed strange and unnecessary at the time now made perfect sense.

Jack felt a sense of pride in his work. He knew that what he was doing was illegal, but he also believed that he was providing a valuable service. He was helping people in desperate situations, giving them a chance to move on with their lives. And in doing so, he was honoring his father's legacy, carrying on the family tradition in his own way.

As he prepared for his next job, Jack knew that the road ahead would be filled with challenges and dangers. But he was ready. He had found his calling, and he was determined to be the best cleaner he could be.

Chapter 4
The Detective's Suspicion

Detective Sam Collins was known for his sharp mind and keen intuition. He was a seasoned detective with a reputation for solving even the most complex cases. For years, he had been quietly investigating a series of murders that seemed too perfectly staged, too meticulously cleaned. The victims varied—cheating spouses, business rivals, accidental overdoses—but the common thread was an eerie cleanliness to the crime scenes, a precision that suggested someone was covering their tracks expertly.

Collins had his suspicions. He believed there was someone out there, a professional cleaner, who specialized in making murders look like accidents, suicides, or unrelated crimes. But despite his instincts, he had no concrete evidence. The cleaner, whoever they were, was a ghost, leaving no trace of their involvement.

Determined to uncover the truth, Collins spent countless nights poring over old case files. He analyzed the crime scenes of murders that were declared accidental deaths or suicides, looking for patterns. He noted the similarities in the way evidence was handled, the way scenes were staged. But the cleaner was too good, always staying a step ahead, erasing every possible clue.

Collins's obsession with the cleaner grew. He became more determined with each passing day, driven by the need to solve the puzzle. His colleagues doubted his theories, but Collins didn't care. He knew the cleaner was real, and he was determined to prove it, no matter how long it took.

Chapter 5
The First Clue

One night, Collins stumbled upon a case that piqued his interest. Clara had reported a robbery gone wrong, resulting in her husband's death. The scene was chaotic, but something about it felt off to Collins. The break-in seemed too staged, the signs of struggle too deliberate. He decided to dig deeper.

He interviewed Clara multiple times, noting her inconsistencies and nervous behavior. She seemed genuine in her grief, but there was something she was hiding. Collins examined the forensic reports, looking for any overlooked detail. And then, he found it—a single, faint fingerprint on the underside of a broken vase. It wasn't much, but it was a start. The print didn't match Clara's or her husband's, nor did it match any known criminals in the database.

Collins felt a surge of excitement. This was the first tangible clue that the cleaner might exist. He expanded his investigation, looking into other cases with similar meticulousness. He found more faint clues—unidentified prints, traces of unusual cleaning agents, signs of staged scenes. Slowly, a pattern emerged, confirming his suspicions.

Chapter 6
The Cleaner's Challenge

Jack, the cleaner, had always been careful. He prided himself on his precision, on his ability to leave no trace. But as he took on more jobs, the pressure mounted, and small mistakes began to slip through. The faint fingerprint on the vase was one such mistake, a rare lapse in his otherwise perfect record.

Jack, however, quickly learned from his mistake. He adjusted his methods, becoming even more meticulous and ensuring he left no evidence behind. He changed his cleaning agents, used new techniques to disguise his tracks, and became even more cautious in his planning.

Despite his increased efforts, Jack couldn't help but feel a sense of respect for the detective who had come so close to discovering him. He followed Collins's investigations from a distance, always staying one step ahead, but acknowledging the detective's tenacity and intelligence. Jack knew that Collins was a worthy adversary, someone who could potentially uncover his identity if he made another mistake.

Jack's respect for Collins grew as he watched the detective's relentless pursuit. He admired Collins's dedication and skill, but he also knew that he had to stay vigilant. The cat-and-mouse game between them had begun, and Jack was determined to stay ahead.

Chapter 7
Collins's Determination

As Collins pieced together the evidence, he knew he was on the right track. He started to notice the cleaner's adjustments, realizing that his investigation was causing the cleaner to evolve. Collins was both frustrated and invigorated by the challenge. He knew he was getting closer, but the cleaner was always just out of reach.

Collins decided to set a trap. He leaked information about a high-profile case, hoping to lure the cleaner into making a move. He monitored the crime scene closely, ensuring that every detail was documented and scrutinized. But Jack, ever cautious, sensed the trap and stayed away, watching from the shadows as Collins waited in vain.

Collins's colleagues continued to doubt his theories, but he remained undeterred. He spent hours analyzing crime scene photos, forensic reports, and witness statements, looking for any clue that could lead him to the cleaner. He knew that one mistake, one slip-up, could be the break he needed.

Chapter 8
The Ongoing Battle

Collins continued his quest, his obsession with catching the cleaner growing with each passing day. He dedicated himself to learning everything he could about crime scene cleaning, forensic science, and criminal psychology. He attended conferences, consulted experts, and even went undercover to learn the tricks of the trade.

Despite his efforts, the cleaner remained elusive. Jack continued his work, always adapting, always staying ahead. The two men were locked in an intricate dance, each one pushing the other to new heights of skill and cunning.

Collins's colleagues still doubted his theories, but he didn't care. He knew the cleaner was real, and he was determined to prove it, no matter how long it took. He was willing to spend his entire career chasing this ghost if necessary.

Jack, for his part, continued to respect Collins's tenacity. He knew that one day, the detective might get close enough to pose a real threat. But until then, he would continue his work, perfecting his craft and staying twenty steps ahead.

Chapter 9
The Legacy

Years passed, and Collins's pursuit of the cleaner became legendary within the police force. New detectives joined the department, inspired by his dedication and his refusal to give up. Collins trained them, passing on his knowledge and his suspicions, hoping that one day, someone would finally catch the cleaner.

Jack, meanwhile, continued his work, taking on fewer jobs but ensuring that each one was executed flawlessly. He knew that Collins would never stop looking for him, and he found a strange comfort in that. Their ongoing battle became a part of his life, a constant reminder to stay sharp, stay hidden, and stay ahead.

The cleaner and the detective—two sides of the same coin, locked in an endless struggle, each one pushing the other to new heights of skill and determination. Neither one would ever truly win, but neither one would ever truly lose. They were destined to play this game forever, each one a step ahead and a step behind, in a dance of shadows and light.

Chapter 10
The High-Profile Cases

Jack's reputation as the cleaner grew, and he began to attract high-profile clients. One day, he received a call from a desperate man who identified himself as a close advisor to the president. A scandal was about to erupt—a powerful senator had been found dead in a hotel room, and the circumstances pointed to a compromising affair and drug overdose.

Jack knew this was no ordinary cleanup. The stakes were higher, and the scrutiny would be intense. He carefully planned his approach, arriving at the scene disguised as hotel staff. The hotel was a luxurious establishment, frequented by politicians and celebrities, making it a high-security area. Jack had to navigate through security checkpoints and surveillance cameras, using his skills to blend in and avoid detection.

He used his knowledge of forensic science to carefully remove any trace of the senator's illicit activities. He replaced the drugs with prescription medication and staged the scene to look like a natural death. Jack meticulously cleaned the room, wiping down every surface, disposing of any potential evidence, and ensuring that no trace of his presence remained.

Jack's meticulous work paid off. The media reported the senator's death as a tragic but natural passing, and the scandal was averted. The advisor was grateful, paying Jack handsomely and promising future referrals. Jack's network of high-profile clients expanded, and he found himself cleaning up after CEOs, celebrities, and even royalty.

Chapter 11
The Presidential Cleanup

One evening, Jack received a call that would challenge his skills like never before. The President of the country was implicated in a scandal involving a young intern found dead in a private residence. The advisor, who had previously contacted Jack, urgently requested his services. The potential fallout from this incident was immense, and the advisor stressed the need for absolute discretion.

Jack meticulously prepared for the cleanup. He donned a sophisticated disguise and gathered advanced forensic tools to ensure no trace of his presence would be left behind. Upon arriving at the scene, Jack observed the chaos and tension among the staff and security personnel. He remained calm, methodically erasing all evidence that could link the President to the intern's death.

Jack carefully cleaned the scene, removing any signs of foul play and planting evidence to suggest a natural death. He knew this cleanup had to be flawless, as the investigation would be intense. The next day, news outlets reported the death as a tragic accident, and the potential scandal was averted. Jack's work had once again saved a high-profile client from disaster.

Chapter 12
The Detective's Breakthrough

Detective Collins, meanwhile, had been tirelessly studying high-profile cases with suspiciously clean crime scenes. The recent death of the senator had piqued his interest, and now the intern's death involving the President raised further suspicions. Collins began to see a pattern—a methodical, precise approach that was too consistent to be coincidental.

Collins cross-referenced these cases, noting the similarities in the cleanup and the lack of forensic evidence. He started to build a profile of the cleaner, theorizing about their methods and motives. Collins's investigation was becoming more focused, and he was determined to catch the cleaner, even if it meant going against powerful figures.

Chapter 13
The Art Gallery Heist

Jack's next job involved a high-profile art gallery owner who had inadvertently killed a rival during a heated argument. The gallery owner panicked and called Jack for help. This cleanup required not only removing the body but also staging the scene to look like a botched heist.

Jack arrived at the gallery and assessed the situation. The gallery was filled with priceless artworks, security systems, and surveillance cameras. Jack had to be extra cautious to avoid being caught on tape. He carefully moved the body and staged a break-in, ensuring that valuable pieces were strategically damaged or stolen. He then planted evidence to implicate a known art thief, creating a convincing narrative for the police. The media reported the incident as a robbery gone wrong, and the gallery owner was relieved.

Chapter 14
The Unseen Footprint

Detective Collins continued to dig deeper into the cleaner's work. He started to notice small, seemingly insignificant details that others had overlooked. In the art gallery case, he found a faint footprint near the scene, partially covered by dust. It was almost as if the cleaner had left it there deliberately, a subtle challenge.

Collins analyzed the footprint and found it didn't match any known suspects. He began to piece together the cleaner's MO—always meticulous, always a step ahead. Collins's determination grew, and he knew he was getting closer, but the cleaner was still an enigma, always twenty steps ahead.

Chapter 15
The Tech Mogul's Secret

Jack received a call from a tech mogul who had accidentally killed his business partner during a confrontation. The mogul was terrified of the potential fallout and called Jack to clean up the mess. Jack understood the importance of handling this case with utmost care, given the mogul's high profile.

Jack arrived at the mogul's penthouse and assessed the scene. The penthouse was a marvel of modern technology, filled with smart devices and security systems. Jack had to disable the security systems and ensure that no digital evidence would be left behind. He carefully removed the body and used advanced technology to erase any digital evidence of the confrontation. He then staged the scene to look like an accidental fall from the balcony. The media reported the death as a tragic accident, and the mogul was safe from scrutiny.

Chapter 16
The Detective's Obsession

Collins's obsession with the cleaner grew. He was now convinced that there was a professional cleaner working behind the scenes, covering up high-profile crimes. He spent nights analyzing crime scenes, cross-referencing cases, and building a profile of the cleaner. He even began to suspect that the cleaner had access to advanced forensic knowledge and technology.

Collins's colleagues thought he was chasing a ghost, but he knew he was onto something. He decided to set another trap, this time involving a fake high-profile crime. He leaked information about a wealthy socialite planning a risky business deal, hoping to lure the cleaner into action.

Chapter 17
The Socialite's Dilemma

Jack received a call from a distressed socialite who had accidentally killed her lover during a heated argument. She feared the scandal and called Jack for help. Unbeknownst to Jack, this was part of Collins's trap. The scene was carefully staged, with hidden surveillance set up by the police.

Jack arrived and began his work, unaware of the surveillance. He meticulously cleaned the scene, removed evidence, and staged it to look like a robbery gone wrong. As he was finishing, he noticed something odd—a faint glimmer of a hidden camera. Jack quickly adjusted his plan, disabling the camera and leaving behind a misleading trail.

Chapter 18
The Near Miss

Collins watched the surveillance feed anxiously, hoping to catch the cleaner in the act. To his frustration, the feed cut out just as the cleaner was finishing the job. When Collins arrived at the scene, he found only misleading evidence and no clear trace of the cleaner.

Collins was both frustrated and impressed. The cleaner had evaded his trap, once again staying ahead. But the detective knew he was getting closer. He analyzed the false trail left by the cleaner, trying to learn more about their methods.

Chapter 19
The Cleaner's Masterpiece

Jack's next job was his most challenging yet—a high-profile politician was involved in a scandalous affair that had ended in murder. The politician's career and reputation were on the line, and Jack was called to clean up the mess. This job required not only removing the body but also erasing any digital and physical evidence of the affair.

Jack meticulously planned the cleanup, using his advanced forensic knowledge to remove all traces of the crime. He staged the scene to look like a natural death, carefully manipulating the evidence to ensure the politician's innocence. The media reported the death as a tragic accident, and the politician's career was saved.

Chapter 20
The Detective's Revelation

Collins continued to piece together the cleaner's work, analyzing each case with renewed vigor. He started to notice patterns in the cleaner's methods, realizing that the cleaner often left subtle clues—a faint footprint, a misplaced object, a slight trace of cleaning agents.

Collins began to understand that the cleaner was not just erasing evidence but also challenging him, leaving behind hints to test his skills. This revelation fueled Collins's determination, and he vowed to catch the cleaner, no matter how long it took.

Chapter 21
The Unseen Battle

Jack and Collins were locked in an unseen battle, each one pushing the other to new heights of skill and determination. Jack continued his work, always staying ahead, always adapting. He took on fewer jobs, focusing on high-profile clients and ensuring each cleanup was flawless.

Collins, meanwhile, dedicated his life to catching the cleaner. He trained new detectives, passing on his knowledge and suspicions, hoping that one day, someone would finally catch the elusive cleaner. But Jack always stayed twenty steps ahead, a ghost in the shadows, leaving no trace of his presence.

The cleaner and the detective—two sides of the same coin, locked in an endless struggle, each one pushing the other to new heights of skill and determination. Neither one would ever truly win, but neither one would ever truly lose. They were destined to play this game forever, each one a step ahead and a step behind, in a dance of shadows and light.

Chapter 22
The Presidential Clean-Up

Jack's most daring job came when he was called to clean up after a president. A scandal had erupted involving a foreign diplomat who was found dead in the president's private residence. The stakes were higher than ever, and the potential fallout could destabilize the entire nation.

Jack meticulously planned the cleanup, knowing this was his most

challenging job yet. He used his advanced forensic knowledge to erase all traces of the diplomat's presence and staged the scene to look like a medical emergency. The media reported the death as a sudden illness, and the scandal was averted.

Chapter 23
The Detective's Final Play

Collins's investigation had led him to a critical moment. He had pieced together enough evidence to understand the cleaner's methods and motives. He knew the cleaner was meticulous, always staying ahead, but he also knew the cleaner had a pattern—a challenge left for the detective to find.

Collins set his final trap, using a high-profile case involving a tech mogul. He carefully staged the scene, ensuring it was a tempting target for the cleaner. Hidden cameras and forensic experts were on standby, ready to catch the cleaner in the act.

Chapter 24
The Cleaner's Escape

Jack sensed the trap as soon as he arrived. The scene felt off, too perfect, too staged. He quickly adapted, using his skills to leave behind a false trail. He disabled the hidden cameras, manipulated the evidence, and vanished into the night.

When Collins arrived, he found only the false trail, a testament to the cleaner's skill. He knew he had come close, but the cleaner had once again stayed ahead. Collins was both frustrated and impressed, knowing he had been outsmarted.

Chapter 25
The Legacy Continues

Years passed, and Jack continued his work, always staying ahead of Collins and the law. He took on fewer jobs, focusing on high-profile clients and ensuring each cleanup was flawless. Collins, meanwhile, trained new detectives, passing on his knowledge and suspicions, hoping that one day, someone would finally catch the elusive cleaner.

Jack and Collins remained locked in their unseen battle, each one pushing the other to new heights of skill and determination. Their lives had become intertwined in a complex dance of wits, a never-ending pursuit where neither could afford to falter.

Chapter 26
The Billionaire's Secret

Jack's latest client was a reclusive billionaire whose luxurious estate was the scene of a deadly confrontation. The billionaire had accidentally killed a blackmailer who threatened to expose his darkest secrets. The consequences of this exposure were too grave, and the billionaire needed Jack's expertise.

Jack arrived at the sprawling estate under the cover of night, blending seamlessly into the shadows. The crime scene was complex, filled with security cameras, advanced alarm systems, and a staff that couldn't know what was happening. Jack disabled the security systems, ensuring no footage of his presence would be left.

He meticulously removed all traces of the blackmailer's presence, staging the scene to appear as if the blackmailer had never been there. Jack used sophisticated chemical cleaners to erase bloodstains and other evidence, and he planted misleading clues to divert any potential investigation.

When the body was discovered the next day, the death was ruled a natural cause, and the billionaire's secrets remained hidden. Jack's flawless execution of the cleanup cemented his reputation as the best in the business.

Chapter 27
The Relentless Pursuit

Detective Collins had grown older, but his determination had not waned. The cleaner had become his white whale, an obsession that he couldn't shake. Collins continued to pour over cases, looking for the faintest hint that could lead him to the elusive figure.

He started to notice a pattern in the clients that the cleaner took on—high-profile individuals with much to lose. Collins began to compile a list of potential future clients, hoping to predict the cleaner's next move. He set up surveillance on these individuals, hoping to catch the cleaner in the act.

Chapter 28
The Diplomat's Dilemma

Jack's next job involved a foreign diplomat who had accidentally killed an escort in a fit of rage. The diplomat's political career and international relations were at stake, and he desperately needed Jack's help. The diplomat's mansion was a fortress, with heavy security and constant monitoring.

Jack had to employ his most advanced tactics to gain access and execute the cleanup without being detected. He infiltrated the mansion under the guise of a maintenance worker, using forged credentials. Once inside, he carefully avoided the security cameras and the watchful eyes of the staff.

He meticulously cleaned the scene, removing all evidence of the escort's presence and planting false evidence to make it appear as if the diplomat had been alone. Jack's skills in forensic science were put to the test, but he managed to complete the job without leaving a trace.

Chapter 29
The Detective's Discovery

While reviewing surveillance footage from one of his potential future clients, Collins noticed something peculiar. A maintenance worker had been present at the diplomat's mansion the night of the escort's death. The worker's behavior seemed off, too calculated, too precise.

Collins requested additional footage and began to piece together the movements of this worker. Although the worker's identity remained hidden, Collins felt a surge of excitement—this could be the break he had been waiting for. He started to track the maintenance worker's activities, hoping it would lead him to the cleaner.

Chapter 30
The Corporate Cover-Up

Jack's next client was a high-ranking executive who had been involved in a fatal accident with a whistleblower. The executive had been trying to prevent the whistleblower from exposing corporate malfeasance. The company's future and the executive's freedom depended on Jack's expertise.

Jack infiltrated the corporate headquarters under the guise of an IT specialist, using sophisticated technology to bypass security measures. He cleaned the crime scene with surgical precision, ensuring that no evidence linked the executive to the whistleblower's death.

He staged the scene to look like a tragic workplace accident, manipulating the evidence to support this narrative. The media reported the incident as an unfortunate accident, and the executive was free from suspicion.

Chapter 31
The Final Confrontation

Detective Collins's investigation led him to the corporate headquarters, where he reviewed the footage and records of the IT specialist. The specialist's credentials were forged, and Collins knew he was onto something. He set up a sting operation, hoping to catch the cleaner during his next job.

Jack, always cautious, sensed the increased scrutiny. He carefully planned his next move, aware that the detective was closing in. Jack decided to take on one last job before disappearing for good—a cleanup for a powerful mafia boss whose heir had been killed in a power struggle.

Jack executed the cleanup flawlessly, but as he was finishing, he noticed subtle signs of a trap. He quickly adapted, leaving behind misleading evidence and slipping away just as Collins and his team arrived.

Chapter 32
The Legacy

Jack knew it was time to disappear. He had pushed his luck to the limit, and Collins was too close for comfort. Jack used his skills to create a new identity, erasing all traces of his previous life. He left behind his legacy, a series of meticulously cleaned crime scenes that would baffle investigators for years to come.

Detective Collins, despite never catching the cleaner, had left a legacy of his own. He trained a new generation of detectives, passing on his knowledge and techniques. His relentless pursuit of the cleaner had made him a legend in the police force, inspiring others to continue the hunt.

Chapter 33
The Ghosts in the Shadows

Years later, whispers of the cleaner's work still echoed in the halls of power. High-profile individuals continued to engage in risky behaviors, knowing that someone, somewhere, could clean up their mess. Jack had become a ghost, a myth that lived on in the shadows.

Collins, now retired, reflected on his career. He never caught the cleaner, but he knew he had come closer than anyone else ever would. He found solace in the knowledge that he had pushed the boundaries of detective work, inspiring others to strive for the same.

Jack, living under his new identity, watched from afar as the world moved on. He knew that his work had left a mark, that his skills were unmatched. He found peace in the quiet, knowing that he had played his part in the dance of shadows and light.

The cleaner and the detective—two sides of the same coin, forever locked in an intricate dance, each pushing the other to new heights of skill and determination. Their story would be told for generations, a testament to the complexity of the human mind and the endless pursuit of perfection.

Chapter 34
The Unsolvable Puzzle

Jack had been living a quiet life, but the thrill of the game still called to him. He decided to take on one last job, not for money, but for the challenge. This time, he would craft a murder so intricate that even his readers would struggle to solve it.

The Client

A famous author, Evelyn Blake, had been blackmailed by her jealous rival, William Hart. William threatened to ruin her reputation and expose her secrets unless she paid him a substantial sum. In a fit of rage, Evelyn accidentally killed William during a heated argument in her study.

The Setup

Evelyn, panicked and desperate, reached out to Jack. She explained the situation, begging for his help to cover up the murder. Jack agreed, seeing this as the perfect opportunity to create an unsolvable puzzle.

The Scene

William's body lay sprawled on the floor of Evelyn's study, a broken vase nearby indicating a struggle. Blood had splattered across the antique rug, and Evelyn's fingerprints were all over the scene.

Jack's Plan

Jack meticulously planned the cleanup, intending to leave just enough clues to confound anyone who tried to solve the mystery. Here's how he did it:

1. Erasing Fingerprints: Jack carefully wiped down all surfaces, removing Evelyn's fingerprints. He then used gloves to place new, indistinguishable prints around the room, creating a mix of possibilities.
2. Planting Evidence: Jack planted several pieces of misleading evidence:
- A note in William's pocket, hinting at a secret meeting with an unnamed individual.
- A piece of jewelry belonging to a third party, suggesting an affair gone wrong.
- A partially burned letter in the fireplace, with fragments of sentences hinting at a conspiracy.
3. Staging the Scene: Jack rearranged the room to suggest a burglary. He broke a window from the outside and scattered valuables around to make it look like a robbery gone wrong.
4. Manipulating the Timeline: Jack altered the clocks in the house, making it difficult to determine the exact time of death. He also left a digital trail on Evelyn's computer, indicating she was online at the time of the murder.
5. Creating Red Herrings: Jack left subtle clues pointing to multiple potential suspects:

- Evelyn's estranged husband: Jack placed a threatening letter from him in her desk.
- A disgruntled employee: Jack used a fake identity to send threatening emails from a computer in Evelyn's home office.
- A jealous fan: Jack left behind an envelope with fan mail that included disturbing, obsessive messages.

The Challenge

Jack left the scene, confident that his work would baffle any investigator. Now, he invites you, the reader, to solve the mystery. Here are the key pieces of evidence to consider:

1. The broken vase and its location.
2. The note in William's pocket.
3. The piece of jewelry.
4. The partially burned letter.
5. The rearranged valuables and the broken window.
6. The altered clocks.
7. The digital trail on Evelyn's computer.
8. The threatening letter from Evelyn's estranged husband.
9. The threatening emails from the disgruntled employee.
10. The obsessive fan mail.

The Questions

As you delve into this mystery, ask yourself:

1. What was the real motive behind the murder?

2. How did the evidence get planted, and who had access to the study?
3. What does the timeline tell you about the sequence of events?
4. Are there inconsistencies in the staged burglary?
5. What does the note in William's pocket reveal about his relationships?
6. Who would benefit most from William's death?
7. How do the threatening messages tie into the murder?
8. What do the fragments of the burned letter suggest?
9. Is there a connection between the piece of jewelry and any of the suspects?
10. Can the digital trail on Evelyn's computer be trusted?

The Solution

The real challenge lies in deciphering the layers of deception Jack has woven into this puzzle. As you piece together the clues, remember that not everything is as it seems. The answer requires a keen eye for detail and a mind sharp enough to see through the smokescreen.

Happy sleuthing, and may the best detective win.

The Solution: Unraveling the Puzzle

As you sift through the layers of deception, the true story behind William Hart's death begins to emerge. Here's how Jack's carefully crafted puzzle can be unraveled:

The Real Motive

Evelyn Blake killed William Hart in a fit of rage during a heated argument. The motive was simple: blackmail. William had threatened to ruin Evelyn's reputation and expose her secrets unless she paid him a substantial sum.

How the Evidence Got Planted

Jack planted misleading evidence to create multiple potential suspects. Understanding who had access to the study helps narrow down the true events:

1. The Note in William's Pocket: This note was planted by Jack to suggest William had a secret meeting. However, there's no substantial evidence to back this up.
2. The Piece of Jewelry: This belongs to Evelyn's estranged husband, planted by Jack to frame him.
3. The Partially Burned Letter: The letter hints at a conspiracy but is too vague to pinpoint a clear suspect. It's a deliberate red herring.

The Staged Burglary

Jack broke a window from the outside and scattered valuables to make it look like a burglary. However, the broken glass would have been on the inside if it were a real break-in. This inconsistency points to the burglary being staged.

The Altered Timeline

Jack altered the clocks and created a digital trail to confuse the time of death. The key is to focus on the digital trail on Evelyn's computer. If she was online at the time of the murder, it suggests she couldn't have done it. However, Jack's manipulation of the timeline makes this unreliable.

The Red Herrings

1. The Threatening Letter: From Evelyn's estranged husband, this letter is planted to mislead. His alibi checks out, removing him from the list of suspects.
2. Threatening Emails: Sent from a computer in Evelyn's home office, these emails were another of Jack's diversions. They lack credibility due to the fake identity used.
3. Obsessive Fan Mail: This envelope is another misleading clue. There's no concrete link between the fan and the murder scene.

Key Evidence

1. The Broken Vase: Its location indicates a struggle, confirming an altercation took place.
2. The Rearranged Valuables: These were scattered to suggest a robbery but were left in an unnatural state.
3. The Burned Letter: The fragments hint at a conspiracy but are too vague to be useful.
4. The Jewelry: Belonging to Evelyn's estranged husband, it was planted to frame him.

Piecing It Together

The timeline, when pieced together correctly, suggests Evelyn was home and could have staged the scene. The broken window and scattered valuables are inconsistencies pointing to a staged burglary. The planted evidence (note, jewelry, emails, fan mail) all serve to mislead and complicate the investigation.

The True Sequence of Events

1. Evelyn and William argue in the study.
2. Evelyn kills William in a fit of rage.
3. Evelyn panics and contacts Jack.
4. Jack arrives and stages the scene, planting evidence and altering the timeline to mislead investigators.
5. The broken vase and its location confirm a struggle, aligning with Evelyn's account of events before Jack's intervention.
6. The planted evidence (note, jewelry, emails, fan mail) all point to multiple suspects, creating a complex web of misleading clues.
7. The staged burglary is inconsistent, with the broken glass inside the room and valuables scattered unnaturally.

Conclusion

Evelyn Blake, driven by fear and panic, killed William Hart. Jack's meticulous staging and planting of evidence created an intricate puzzle, but the inconsistencies in the burglary and the timeline manipulation ultimately revealed the truth. The digital trail, while misleading, indicated Evelyn's presence at the time of the murder, and the broken vase and valuables confirmed the scene was staged.

In the end, Evelyn's guilt is evident, but Jack's clever misdirections made the puzzle challenging to solve. His final job was a testament to his skill, leaving a legacy of unsolved mysteries and intricate deceptions.

Interactive Puzzle: Take Control of Jack

Welcome to the next challenge! In this interactive puzzle, you will step into Jack's shoes and make decisions to clean up a crime scene. Your goal is to cover all traces of the murder and avoid detection. Let's see if you have what it takes to be the ultimate cleaner.

The Scenario

A prominent CEO, Marcus Thompson, has been found dead in his penthouse apartment. He was hosting a high-stakes business meeting with five attendees. After the meeting, Marcus was found dead with a bullet wound to the head. Your client, one of the attendees, accidentally shot Marcus during a heated argument and needs your help to cover it up.

The Crime Scene

- Location: Marcus Thompson's penthouse.
- Victim: Marcus Thompson, shot in the head.

- Witnesses: Five business associates, all present during the meeting.
- Time Frame: You have three hours before the police arrive.

Steps to Clean the Scene

You will need to make choices at each step. Based on your decisions, the outcome will vary. Choose wisely!

Step 1: Enter the Scene

Option A: Enter through the front door.

- Risk: You might be seen by neighbors or security cameras.

Option B: Enter through the service entrance.

- Risk: Limited access, but less likely to be seen.

Step 2: Deal with the Witnesses

Option A: Intimidate the witnesses to ensure their silence.

- Risk: They might not comply or could betray you later.

Option B: Offer the witnesses money to keep quiet.

- Risk: Expensive and not foolproof.

Option C: Disguise yourself and leave unnoticed.

- Risk: Requires a perfect disguise and timing.

Step 3: Clean the Blood

   Option A: Use professional cleaning agents to remove bloodstains.

- Risk: Time-consuming but thorough.

   Option B: Replace the stained carpet and clean the visible surfaces.

- Risk: Faster, but might leave traces.

Step 4: Dispose of the Body

   Option A: Move the body to a hidden location within the building.

- Risk: Difficult to transport without being seen.

   Option B: Stage the scene to look like a suicide.

- Risk: Requires precise staging and a believable narrative.

   Option C: Arrange for a discreet removal service.

- Risk: Expensive and requires trusted contacts.

Step 5: Alter the Evidence

   Option A: Wipe all fingerprints and leave no trace.
- Risk: Thorough but time-consuming.

Option B: Plant false evidence to mislead investigators.

- Risk: Requires detailed knowledge of forensic procedures.

Option C: Erase all digital evidence (security footage, emails).

- Risk: Can be complicated and might raise suspicion if done poorly.

Step 6: Create an Alibi for Your Client

Option A: Forge time-stamped evidence placing your client elsewhere.

- Risk: Requires access to digital records and precision.

Option B: Arrange for witnesses to vouch for your client's location.

- Risk: Unreliable and might not hold up under scrutiny.

Make Your Choices

Think carefully about each step and how it affects the overall outcome. Your decisions will determine if the crime scene is successfully cleaned without leaving a trace or if critical mistakes are made, leading to Jack's exposure.

Submit Your Actions

Write down your sequence of actions and submit them. Compare your approach with others to see who did the best job at cleaning up the crime scene.

Conclusion

Based on your decisions, you will receive feedback on how well you performed the clean-up. Did you cover all traces, or were there mistakes that could lead to discovery? The best strategy will be showcased, highlighting the most efficient and clever methods of crime scene cleaning.

Good luck, and let's see if you have what it takes to step into Jack's shoes and become the ultimate cleaner!

This interactive puzzle not only engages readers but also challenges them to think like Jack. By making strategic decisions, they can see how well they handle the complexities of a crime scene clean-up.

Interactive Puzzle: The Detective's Challenge

Welcome to the next interactive challenge! In this puzzle, you will step into the shoes of Detective Liam Carter, tasked with uncovering evidence against the elusive cleaner, Jack. Your goal is to find clues that lead you to Jack, but beware: Jack is always twenty steps ahead. Only the smartest and most observant players will come close to finding any evidence.

The Scenario

Detective Liam Carter has been investigating a series of suspiciously clean crime scenes. Each case leaves no evidence behind, but Carter suspects there is a professional cleaner involved. Your task is to gather evidence to prove this theory.

Case in Focus: The murder of CEO Marcus Thompson.

The Crime Scene

- Location: Marcus Thompson's penthouse.
- Victim: Marcus Thompson, shot in the head.
- Witnesses: Five business associates, all present during the meeting.
- Initial Observations: The scene looks like a suicide, but Carter knows something is off.

Steps to Investigate

You will need to make strategic choices at each step. Based on your decisions, the outcome will vary. Choose wisely and see if you can outsmart Jack!

Step 1: Examine the Crime Scene

Option A: Inspect the area for hidden bloodstains using Luminol.
- Risk: Jack is thorough; this might yield nothing.

Option B: Search for inconsistencies in the staged suicide.
- Risk: Requires a keen eye for detail.

Option C: Collect all electronic devices for forensic analysis.
- Risk: Time-consuming and might not lead to immediate clues.

Step 2: Interview the Witnesses

Option A: Apply pressure and look for inconsistencies in their stories.
- Risk: Witnesses might be scared into silence.

Option B: Offer immunity for truthful information.
- Risk: Expensive and might still not yield results.

Option C: Conduct covert surveillance on the witnesses.
- Risk: Time-intensive but could reveal hidden connections.

Step 3: Analyze the Digital Evidence

    Option A: Examine security footage for anomalies.
- Risk: Jack likely erased or altered key footage.

    Option B: Investigate phone records for suspicious calls.

- Risk: Requires access to secure databases.

    Option C: Search for deleted emails or messages.

- Risk: Could lead to dead ends if Jack used encrypted communication.

Step 4: Follow the Money

    Option A: Trace large transactions in Marcus Thompson's accounts.

- Risk: Might lead to dead ends if Jack used cash.

    Option B: Look for unusual purchases or expenses.

- Risk: Requires detailed financial scrutiny.

    Option C: Investigate the financial background of the witnesses.

- Risk: Time-consuming and might not directly lead to Jack.

Step 5: Collaborate with Forensic Experts

Option A: Request a detailed forensic report on the crime scene.

- Risk: Jack's methods might leave no forensic evidence.

Option B: Consult with a criminal profiler to understand Jack's pattern.

- Risk: Profiles can be abstract and might not lead to concrete evidence.

Option C: Engage a digital forensic specialist to uncover hidden data.

- Risk: Expensive and might not yield actionable results.

Make Your Choices

Think carefully about each step and how it affects the overall investigation. Your decisions will determine if you can get closer to finding evidence against Jack or if he remains an enigma, always one step ahead.

Submit Your Investigation

Write down your sequence of actions and submit them. Compare your approach with others to see who came closest to uncovering any clues about Jack's involvement.

Conclusion

Based on your decisions, you will receive feedback on how well you performed the investigation. Did you uncover any critical clues, or did Jack remain a ghost, leaving no trace behind? The best strategies will be showcased, highlighting the most persistent and clever investigative methods.

Good luck, and let's see if you can step into Detective Carter's shoes and come close to catching the ultimate cleaner!

This interactive puzzle not only engages readers but also challenges them to think like a detective. By making strategic decisions, they can see how well they handle the complexities of investigating a crime scene and trying to catch someone as elusive as Jack.

Interactive Feature: Design Your Own Mystery

We invite you to unleash your creativity and craft your own murder mystery! Share your story online and challenge others to solve it. This feature allows you to design intricate crime scenes, develop compelling characters, and create twists and turns that will keep the community engaged and guessing. Follow the steps below to create and share your unique murder mystery.

Steps to Create Your Own Murder Mystery

1. Craft the Crime Scene

Location: Choose a unique setting for your murder.

- Options: Abandoned mansion, bustling city street, secluded cabin, luxurious yacht, etc.

Victim: Describe the victim and their background.

- Options: Wealthy businessman, famous artist, local politician, mysterious stranger, etc.

Method: Specify how the murder was committed.

- Options: Poisoning, stabbing, shooting, strangulation, etc.

2. Develop the Characters

Suspects: Create a list of suspects with detailed backgrounds and motives.

- Suspect 1: Describe their relationship with the victim and potential motive.
- Suspect 2: Provide a brief history and reason for suspicion.
- Suspect 3: Outline their behavior and possible connection to the crime.

Witnesses: Include any witnesses who might have seen something crucial.

- Describe what they saw and their reliability.

3. Plant the Clues

Physical Evidence: List any physical evidence found at the crime scene.

- Options: Bloody knife, fingerprints, mysterious letter, broken window, etc.

Red Herrings: Add false clues to mislead and challenge the readers.

- Options: Misleading statements, irrelevant objects, false testimonies, etc.

Hidden Clues: Include subtle hints that lead to the real murderer.

- Options: Hidden messages, overlooked details, connections between suspects, etc.

4. Write the Story

Introduction: Set the scene and introduce the characters.

Body: Develop the plot, include clues and red herrings.

Conclusion: Reveal the murderer and explain how the clues led to the conclusion.

5. Share Your Mystery

Platform: Choose where to share your story online.

- Options: Social media (Instagram, TikTok), dedicated mystery forums, your personal blog, etc.

Engagement: Encourage readers to submit their solutions.
- Ask them to explain their reasoning and how they connected the clues.
- Provide feedback on the best solutions and highlight creative approaches.

Example: Create Your Own Murder Mystery

Title: "The Silent Killer"

Location: A lavish party at a seaside villa.

Victim: Emma Cross, a renowned novelist.

Method: Poisoned champagne.

Suspects:

1. James Ryder: Emma's jealous ex-husband, seen arguing with her before her death.
2. Sophia Lane: A fellow writer who envied Emma's success.

3. Victor Hale: The villa owner who had a secret past with Emma.

Witnesses:

- Lucy Hart: The party planner who saw a mysterious figure near the bar.
- Daniel Smith: A waiter who overheard a heated conversation between Emma and Sophia.

Physical Evidence:

- A half-empty champagne bottle with traces of poison.
- Emma's diary with cryptic entries.
- A broken bracelet near the bar.

Red Herrings:

- A threatening letter found in Emma's room.
- James's fingerprints on the champagne glass.
- An anonymous phone call warning Emma days before the party.

Hidden Clues:

- The diary entries contain coded messages about Emma's fear of being poisoned.
- The broken bracelet belongs to Lucy Hart, who had access to the bar area.
- Victor Hale's connection to a pharmaceutical company producing the poison.

Share Your Mystery:

- Post your mystery on Instagram with the hashtag MysteryChallenge.
- Encourage readers to submit their solutions in the comments or through direct messages.
- Feature the best solutions and provide feedback on the most insightful deductions.

Engage with the Community

Chapter 35
The Journalist's Curiosity

Years had passed since Jack had vanished into the shadows, living under a new identity. Despite his efforts to remain hidden, whispers of his work continued to circulate among those in the know. One day, Jack received an unexpected visitor: a young investigative journalist named Sarah Greene. She had spent years piecing together fragments of stories about the mysterious cleaner and was determined to uncover the truth.

Sarah had tracked down Jack's old life, following a trail of obscure references and tenuous connections. She knocked on the door of his quiet suburban home, her heart pounding with anticipation. Jack opened the door, his face expressionless but his eyes sharp and alert.

Can I help you?" he asked, his voice steady.

Mr. Adams," Sarah began, using Jack's new alias. "I'm Sarah Greene, an investigative journalist. I've been following a story for years, and I believe you can help me."

Jack's mind raced. He knew the risks of engaging with anyone who might expose him, but he was also curious about how much she knew. "I'm not sure what you're talking about," he said, his tone carefully neutral.

Sarah smiled slightly, sensing his hesitation. "I've been researching a series of meticulously cleaned crime scenes. I believe there's someone out there, a professional cleaner, who makes murders look like accidents or suicides. I think you know something about this."

Jack studied her for a moment before stepping aside. "Come in," he said, deciding to hear her out. He led her to the living room, where they sat down. "What makes you think I'm involved?"

Sarah pulled out a folder filled with documents and photos. "I've connected the dots between several high-profile cases. There are patterns, subtle but consistent. I've also spoken to Detective Sam Collins, who spent years trying to catch the cleaner. He believes the cleaner left hints for him, almost as if it was a game."

Jack felt a pang of nostalgia at the mention of Collins. He respected the detective's tenacity and intelligence, but he had always managed to stay ahead. "Collins is a good detective," Jack said. "But why come to me?"

Sarah leaned forward, her eyes intense. "Because I think you're the cleaner. You disappeared around the same time the cleaner stopped taking new jobs. The patterns, the meticulous nature of the work—it all points to you."

Jack felt a surge of adrenaline. This young journalist was smart, and she had come dangerously close to uncovering his identity. He had two options: deny everything and hope she went away or embrace the challenge and guide her investigation. "Let's say, hypothetically, that I am the cleaner," he said carefully. "What do you want from me?"

Sarah's eyes lit up. "I want to tell your story. The truth, from your perspective. Why you did it, how you did it, and what drove you to become the cleaner. In return, I promise to keep your identity anonymous."

Jack considered her offer. He had always been careful to protect his identity, but the idea of his story being told intrigued him. "I'll think about it," he said finally. "But if I agree, there will be conditions."

Sarah nodded eagerly. "Of course. Whatever it takes."

Chapter 36
The Confession

Over the next few weeks, Jack and Sarah met several times, each meeting a careful dance of trust and caution. Jack revealed small details about his past, testing Sarah's commitment and integrity. He spoke about his father's training, the first job with Clara, and the meticulous techniques he had developed over the years.

Sarah listened intently, taking notes and asking insightful questions. She was fascinated by Jack's story, the duality of his life as a cleaner and the meticulous nature of his work. "Why did you do it?" she asked one evening, as they sat in Jack's living room. "Why take on such a dangerous profession?"

Jack leaned back, his expression contemplative. "It started as a way to honor my father's legacy. He trained me without my knowing, and after he died, I felt a responsibility to continue his work. But over time, it became more than that. I realized I was good at it, and there was a certain thrill in staying ahead of the law."

"But didn't you ever feel guilty?" Sarah pressed. "Knowing you were helping people get away with murder?"

Jack sighed. "Of course. There were nights I couldn't sleep, haunted by the faces of the victims. But I justified it by telling myself I was helping people in desperate situations. I was providing a service that no one else could."

Sarah nodded, understanding the complex morality Jack grappled with. "And Detective Collins? What was your relationship with him like?"

Jack smiled faintly. "Collins was my greatest adversary. He was relentless, always one step behind. In a way, he made me better, pushed me to refine my techniques. There was a mutual respect, even though he never knew who I was."

As Sarah pieced together Jack's story, she realized the depth of his experiences and the psychological toll it had taken on him. She felt a growing empathy for him, understanding that his actions were driven by a mix of duty, skill, and the thrill of the chase.

Chapter 37
The Final Job

Despite his resolve to stay hidden, Jack couldn't resist the pull of one final job. A high-profile client reached out to him, desperate and willing to pay a substantial sum. The job involved cleaning up after a powerful senator who had accidentally killed his mistress during a heated argument.

Jack meticulously planned the cleanup, knowing that this would be his last. He donned a new disguise and gathered his tools, feeling a familiar rush of adrenaline. As he entered the senator's luxurious penthouse, he was struck by the opulence and the stark contrast to the grim task at hand.

The scene was chaotic—broken furniture, bloodstains, and signs of a struggle. Jack got to work, methodically cleaning the blood, disposing of evidence, and staging the scene to look like a tragic accident. He wiped down every surface, careful not to leave any trace of his presence.

As he finished the cleanup, Jack felt a sense of closure. He had completed his final job, and it was flawless. He left the penthouse, slipping into the night like a shadow, knowing that his legacy as the cleaner was secure.

Chapter 38
The Unseen Battle

Detective Collins, now retired, had never stopped thinking about the cleaner. He had followed Sarah Greene's investigation with interest, recognizing her determination and intelligence. One evening, he received an unexpected call from Sarah.

"Detective Collins," she said, her voice filled with urgency. "I think I've found the cleaner."

Collins's heart raced. "What do you mean?"

"I've been interviewing someone who fits the profile perfectly," Sarah explained. "He's confessed to several jobs, including some you investigated. I think you should meet him."

Collins agreed, and the next day, he met Sarah and Jack at a secluded location. As he looked into Jack's eyes, he felt a mix of emotions—anger, curiosity, and a grudging respect.

"Jack," Collins said quietly. "You were always just out of reach."

Jack nodded. "I respected you, Collins. You pushed me to be better."

Collins studied Jack for a moment before speaking. "Why now? Why come forward?"

Jack glanced at Sarah before answering. "I wanted my story to be told. The truth, from my perspective. And I'm tired of running."

Collins nodded slowly. "You know what this means, don't you? You'll have to answer for what you've done."

Jack sighed. "I know. But maybe it's time."

Chapter 39
The Disappearance

The following morning, Jack awoke to find a note slipped under his door. It was from Sarah, written in hurried, desperate handwriting.

"Jack, you need to leave. Collins has called in reinforcements, and they're coming for you. I didn't mean for it to go this way. Please, get out while you can."

Jack's heart pounded as he read the note. He had always known this moment could come, but it still hit him with a force he wasn't prepared for. He packed his essentials quickly and slipped out the back door, disappearing into the early morning mist.

Collins arrived shortly after with a team of officers, only to find Jack's home empty. It was as if he had vanished into thin air. Frustration and admiration warred within him. Jack had outsmarted them once again.

Chapter 40
The New Identity

Jack knew he had to disappear for good this time. He utilized all his skills and resources to create a new identity, ensuring that no one would ever trace him again. He moved to a remote village in another country, blending in with the locals and starting a new life.

He kept a low profile, working simple jobs and making new connections. But the thrill of his past life still lingered in the back of his mind. He knew he would never be able to fully escape it, but he was determined to live quietly and anonymously.

Chapter 41
The Legacy

Despite his best efforts to remain hidden, Jack's legend grew. Stories of the cleaner became folklore among criminals and law enforcement alike. His meticulous methods, his ability to stay ahead of the law, and his cunning intelligence made him a mythic figure.

Sarah Greene published a book about her investigation, anonymizing Jack but detailing his exploits. The book became a bestseller, captivating readers with the tale of the mysterious cleaner and his elusive nature.

Detective Collins retired for good, haunted by the one case he could never close. He respected Jack's skills but couldn't shake the feeling of unfinished business. He passed on his knowledge to new detectives, hoping that one day, someone might succeed where he had failed.

Chapter 42
The Call

Years later, in his quiet village, Jack received a call on a burner phone he had kept hidden. It was a voice he hadn't heard in a long time—Sarah Greene.

"Jack," she said, her voice steady. "There's something you need to know. A new cleaner has emerged, and their methods are eerily similar to yours. I think someone is trying to take your place."

Jack felt a chill run down his spine. He had left that life behind, but it seemed it was not done with him. "Where?" he asked simply.

"New York," Sarah replied. "It's big, and they're making waves. I thought you'd want to know."

Jack thanked her and hung up, contemplating his next move. He had thought his story was over, but perhaps it was just beginning a new chapter. He knew he couldn't ignore this challenge. The cleaner might have to return, not to reclaim a throne, but to ensure the legacy was protected.

Chapter 43
The Return

Jack prepared meticulously, just as he always had. He donned a new disguise and made his way to New York. The city was a bustling hive of activity, a far cry from his quiet village. But Jack thrived in the shadows, blending seamlessly into the urban jungle.

He began his investigation, quietly observing and gathering information about the new cleaner. It didn't take long for him to find the first clues—cleaned crime scenes that bore his signature meticulousness but lacked the finesse of his own work.

Jack realized this new cleaner was skilled but reckless, driven more by ambition than the careful precision that had defined his own career. He knew he had to act before this pretender tarnished the legacy he had built.

Chapter 44
The Confrontation

Jack finally tracked down the new cleaner, a young, ambitious man named Alex. They met in a secluded alleyway, the tension palpable.

"You're the cleaner," Alex said, his voice a mix of awe and defiance. "I thought you were a myth."

Jack stepped forward, his gaze steely. "And you're trying to take my place. But you lack the discipline, the precision. You're drawing too much attention."

Alex bristled. "I can handle it. The world has changed. It's faster, more connected. Your methods are outdated."

Jack shook his head. "You don't understand the essence of the work. It's not about speed or fame. It's about perfection, about staying invisible."

The two stood in silence for a moment before Jack spoke again. "I'm giving you a choice. Disappear, or I will make you disappear."

Alex stared at him, weighing his options. He knew he couldn't win against the legend standing before him. "Alright," he said finally. "I'll go."

Jack nodded. "Make sure you do. And never look back."

Chapter 45
The Future

With the new cleaner gone, Jack returned to his quiet life, but the experience had reignited something within him. He realized that his story was far from over. There would always be those who needed his skills, who would seek out the cleaner in times of desperation.

He resumed his work, carefully selecting his clients and ensuring that each job was executed with the same meticulous precision that had made him a legend. He remained a ghost, a myth that lived on in whispers and shadows.

Jack knew that his life would always be a delicate balance between the darkness and the light. But he was ready for whatever challenges lay ahead, knowing that he would always be twenty steps ahead, a master of the shadows.

The cleaner and the detective—two sides of the same coin, forever locked in an intricate dance, each pushing the other to new heights of skill and determination. Their story would continue, a testament to the complexity of the human mind and the endless pursuit of perfection.

Epilogue

Jack sat in his small, quiet home, reflecting on the path he had chosen. The phone on his table buzzed softly, a new message lighting up the screen. He picked it up, reading the brief, coded request. Another job, another challenge.

With a sigh, Jack stood up and began to gather his tools. He knew that he could never fully escape the life he had built, but he was at peace with that. The cleaner's work was never done, and there would always be those who needed his unique skills.

As he stepped out into the night, Jack knew that his story was far from over. He was the cleaner, and the dance of shadows and light would continue, forever entwined in the intricate web of life and death.

End of Book One

Stay tuned for the next installment in the saga of Jack, the cleaner. The legacy continues, and the dance of shadows and light will bring new challenges, new adversaries, and new stories to tell.

Made in the USA
Middletown, DE
01 December 2024